T0392319

THE ANT WHO FOUND THE TRUTH

AUTHOR: JACOB BUTKIEWICZ

To order additional copies of this book, contact:
Xlibris
844-714-8691
www.Xlibris.com
Orders@Xlibris.com

ISBN: Softcover   979-8-3694-2394-3
         Hardcover   979-8-3694-2395-0
         EBook   979-8-3694-2393-6

Library of Congress Control Number: 2024911592

Print information available on the last page

Rev. date: 08/05/2024

SPECIAL THANKS

I like to thank God, Jesus Christ, and the Holy Spirit and the Angels of this Life and The Next. I want to thank my Family and Close Friends that showed Love to me—you all Helped me. I want to thank my Teams I play with and Lead: (1) RUIN—Real Universal Infiltration Network; (2) HAVC—Honorable Armor Victory Committed. I want to thank all encounters; Good or Bad, you can always learn from it. I want to thank artist Mary Rose Aviles. You did a wonderful work. I want to thank Jesus Christ for everything. You are the Best thing that ever happened to me and my Family and Friends' Life. I can never thank you enough, but I Love and Appreciate you for Everything in always being there. John 3:16—"For God so Loved the world that He gave His only begotten Son, that whosoever believeth in Him should not perish but have Everlasting Life." This verse applies to ALL! God Bless you all you and your Families and Loved Ones.

Now all of you, for this Story it's advised to have a Dictionary and Bible handy so you can follow along. Jesus' words will be in red. The Day was 3:16 and Hermin the Ant left his hive to find the meaning of the day by order of the Ant Queen Matilda. Hermin was concerned because none of the other Ants were going with him, only Hermin. Hermin was determined to find the meaning of the number. So Hermin prepared to set off on his quest to find the meaning of John 3:16. Hermin was asked by the other ants why he was going on the quest. He said, "I go because the Queen wants me to go and for the good of the hive." A lot of them doubted him and didn't think he was capable, but unlike them, Hermin had Courage and Heart. Hermin always believed in a Higher Power and was set to one day get there.

Before Hermin left on his Quest, he put on his favorite red hat along with all the gear needed for his trip. Hermin put everything inside his Backpack. Hermin also packed a dictionary. In case he didn't understand a word, he would look it up. Hermin Knew he would be hungry, so he packed a Peanut Butter and Jelly Sandwich, Chocolate Chip Cookies, and Juice in his Lunch pail.

Once Hermin prepared for his quest, he said a prayer, "Please guide me to you in all ways so that I connect to you and you can save my people. Please Give us the Love we are missing." Hermin said goodbye to his family and close friends and was on his way.

Now Hermin liked to travel on moving shoes, so his first encounter was Hudson the Bear. Hermin said, "Hi, can you tell me your job and in three words that best describe what you do?"

So Hudson the Bear said, "I work In a factory making ceramic parts with machines. My three words are: Dedication, Patience, and Determination."

Hermin replied, "Thank You, Hudson the Bear."

Hudson replied, "No problem."

When Hermin was done, he immediately hopped from the shoe he was on to the next shoe.

Hermin looked up and he said, "Hi, what's your name?"

"I'm Esafe the Lion."

"Nice to meet you, Esafe," Hermin said. "What is your job, and three words best describe it?"

"I'm an Airplane Mechanic who makes sure it's safe for planes to fly. My three words are: Rewarding, Integrity, and Challenging. Thanks for asking about my job," Esafe the Lion said to Hermin.

Hermin said, "I appreciate you, Esafe the Lion."

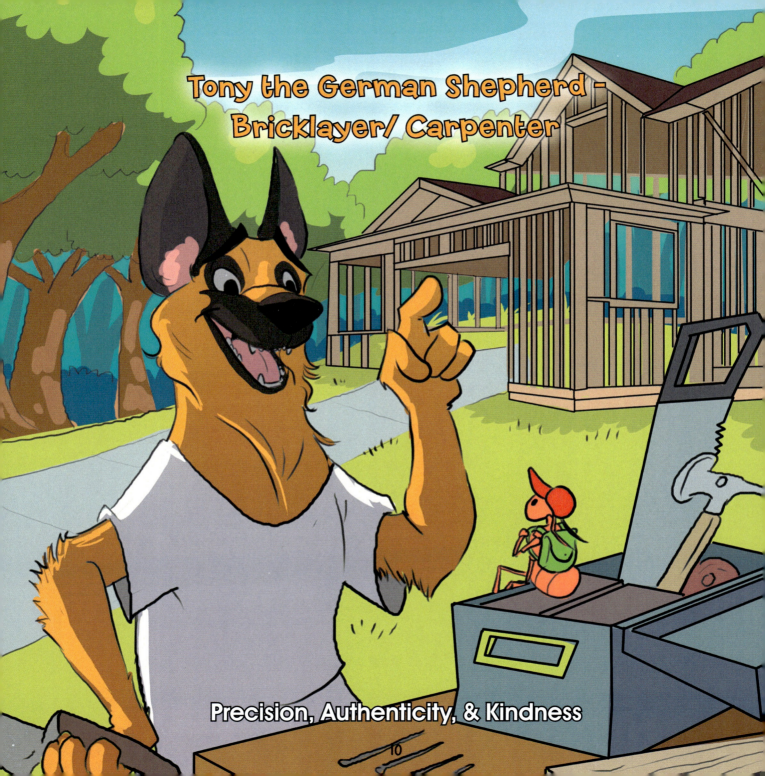

Tony the German Shepherd - Bricklayer/ Carpenter

Precision, Authenticity, & Kindness

In Hermin's next shoe, he came to meet is Tony the German Shepherd.

"How are you doing, Tony?" Hermin Said.

"Just Fine, my Friend, how can I help you?" Tony said.

Hermin replied, "What is your job and what three words that best describe it?"

"I'm a Bricklayer/Carpenter, my three words are: Precision, Authenticity, and Kindness, the joy I have building something that once wasn't there," Said Tony.

"Thank you, Tony," Hermin said.

"My pleasure, my Friend," Tony Said.

Hermin was onto the next shoe; he came across Cruzie the Cheetah.

"Hello, Cruzie, how is your day so far?" Hermin said.

"It's going pretty good, Hermin, can't complain," Cruzie Said.

Hermin asked, "What is your job and three words that best describe it?"

Cruzie replied, "I'm a Baker, I bake goods to the customers preference. My three words are: Adventurous, Kindhearted, and Devoted. Here's a fresh batch of Brownies I made, you can have one, Hermin."

"Thank you so much, Cruzie," Hermin said.

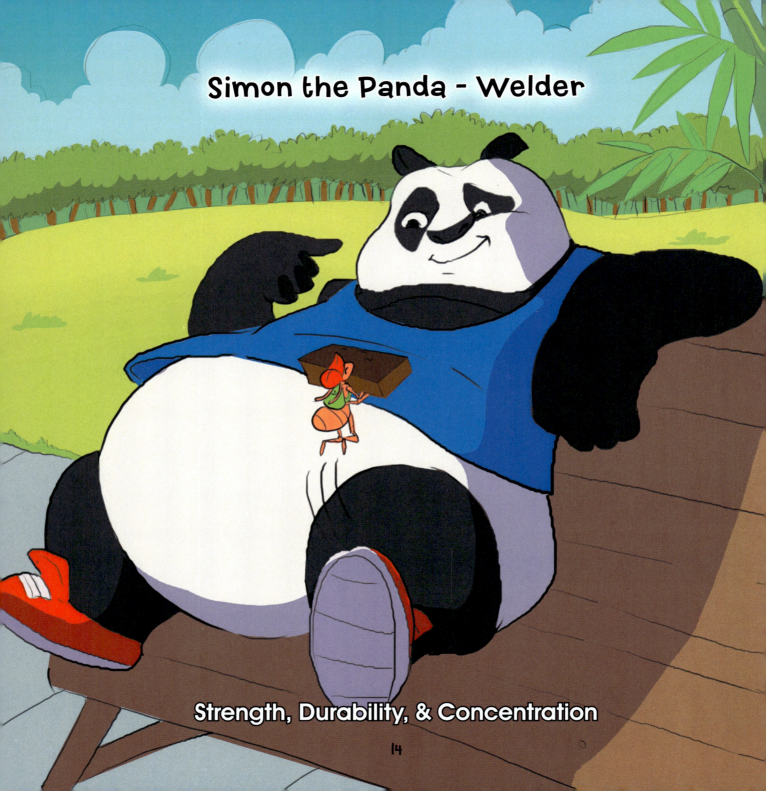

Simon the Panda - Welder

Strength, Durability, & Concentration

Now Hermin took a break to eat part of his Brownie and also went over the words he was told. He was looking for a certain set of words. After taking a small break, he moved forward onto the next shoe. Now Hermin had seen a shoe still, so he leaped up and asked, "How you doing? I'm Hermin the Ant, what's your name?"

"I'm Simon the Panda."

Hermin asked, "What is your job and, in three words, what best describes it?"

"I'm a Welder, I weld pipes together and pressure lines. My three words are: Strength, Durability, and Concentration." Simon asked, "Hey, Mate, do you happen to have anything I can eat?"

Hermin said, "Yes, I have a piece of a Brownie left. You can have it. Here you go," Hermin said and handed Simon his last piece.

Simon said, "Thanks, Mate, you're a Lifesaver."

"Thank you, Simon, I value our connection."

Simon Says, "Same to you, Mate."

Hermin headed to the next shoe.

Now Hermin came across Alex the Penguin.

Alex looked down and said, "What's up? I'm Alex the Penguin, what's your name?"

"I'm Hermin the Ant. Pleased to meet you," Hermin said. "What is your job and, in three words, what best describes it?"

"I'm a Valet Supervisor, I will dictate where employees work throughout the day. My three words are: Nucleus, Leadership, and Fair. Thanks for being Inquisitive about my job," Alex said to Hermin.

Hermin said, "It's my pleasure, Alex." Hermin saw a boot and jumped on it.

Marie the Honey Badger - Law Enforcement Officer

Law, Protection, & Help

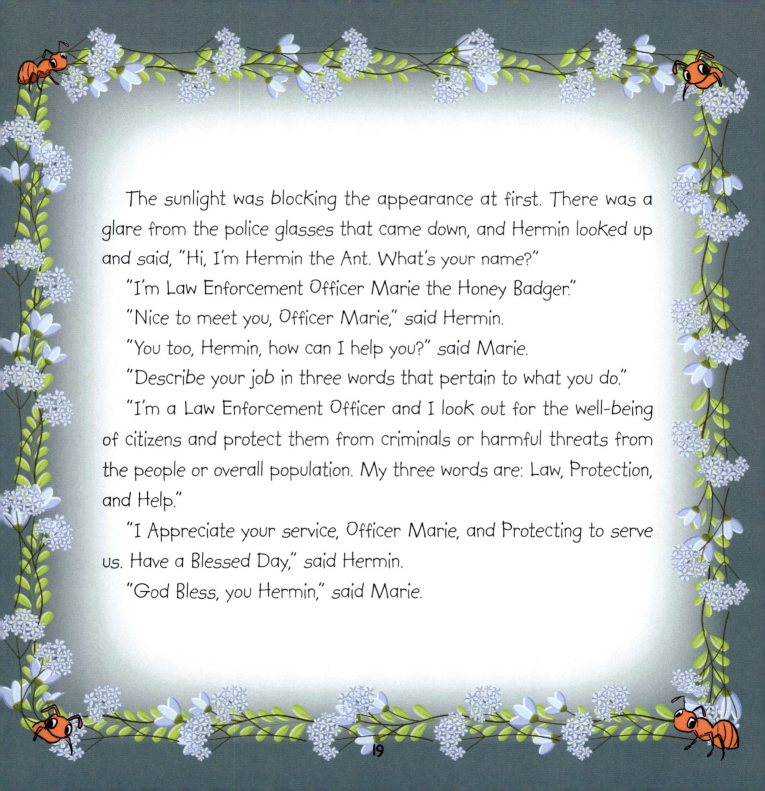

The sunlight was blocking the appearance at first. There was a glare from the police glasses that came down, and Hermin looked up and said, "Hi, I'm Hermin the Ant. What's your name?"

"I'm Law Enforcement Officer Marie the Honey Badger."

"Nice to meet you, Officer Marie," said Hermin.

"You too, Hermin, how can I help you?" said Marie.

"Describe your job in three words that pertain to what you do."

"I'm a Law Enforcement Officer and I look out for the well-being of citizens and protect them from criminals or harmful threats from the people or overall population. My three words are: Law, Protection, and Help."

"I Appreciate your service, Officer Marie, and Protecting to serve us. Have a Blessed Day," said Hermin.

"God Bless, you Hermin," said Marie.

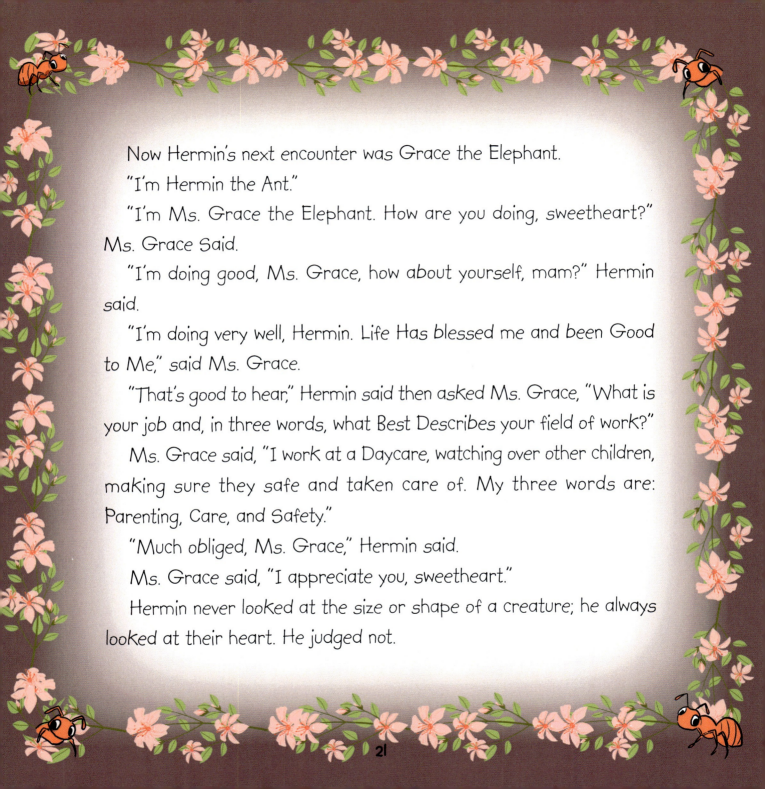

Now Hermin's next encounter was Grace the Elephant.

"I'm Hermin the Ant."

"I'm Ms. Grace the Elephant. How are you doing, sweetheart?" Ms. Grace Said.

"I'm doing good, Ms. Grace, how about yourself, mam?" Hermin said.

"I'm doing very well, Hermin. Life Has blessed me and been Good to Me," said Ms. Grace.

"That's good to hear," Hermin said then asked Ms. Grace, "What is your job and, in three words, what Best Describes your field of work?"

Ms. Grace said, "I work at a Daycare, watching over other children, making sure they safe and taken care of. My three words are: Parenting, Care, and Safety."

"Much obliged, Ms. Grace," Hermin said.

Ms. Grace said, "I appreciate you, sweetheart."

Hermin never looked at the size or shape of a creature; he always looked at their heart. He judged not.

Shash the Calico Cat - Nurse

Open-minded, Communication, & Empathy

22

The next shoe he came across was Shash the Calico Cat.

"Hello, Shash, how are you?" Hermin asked.

"I'm doing good, Hermin," Shash said. "What can I do to help you?"

Hermin said, "What is your job and, in three words, what Best Describes the work you do?"

Shash said, "I'm a Nurse. I look over patients and take care of people. My three words are: Open-minded, Communication, and Empathy. I hope you find what you looking for."

"I have Faith I will," said Hermin.

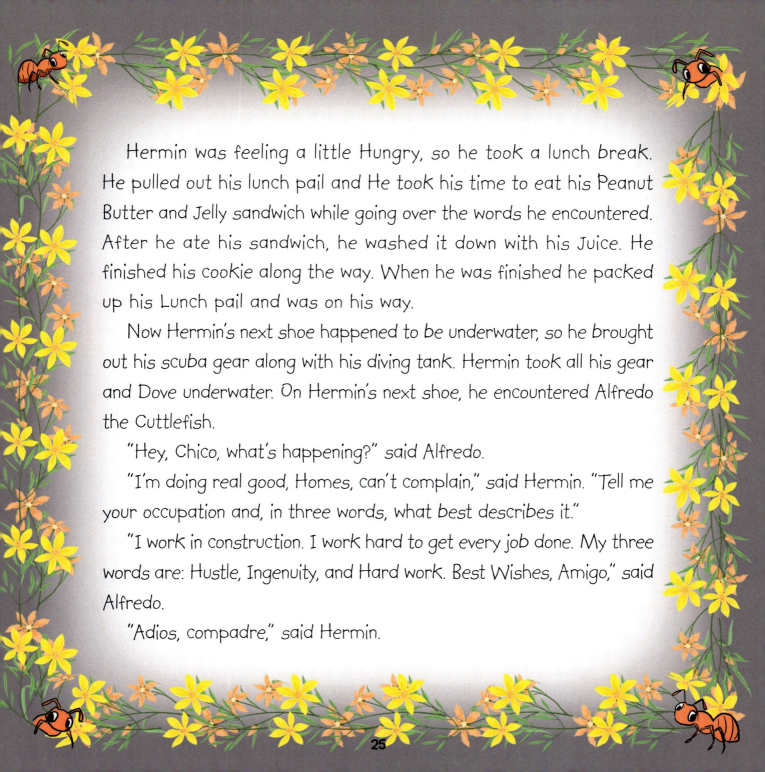

Hermin was feeling a little Hungry, so he took a lunch break. He pulled out his lunch pail and He took his time to eat his Peanut Butter and Jelly sandwich while going over the words he encountered. After he ate his sandwich, he washed it down with his Juice. He finished his cookie along the way. When he was finished he packed up his Lunch pail and was on his way.

Now Hermin's next shoe happened to be underwater, so he brought out his scuba gear along with his diving tank. Hermin took all his gear and Dove underwater. On Hermin's next shoe, he encountered Alfredo the Cuttlefish.

"Hey, Chico, what's happening?" said Alfredo.

"I'm doing real good, Homes, can't complain," said Hermin. "Tell me your occupation and, in three words, what best describes it."

"I work in construction. I work hard to get every job done. My three words are: Hustle, Ingenuity, and Hard work. Best Wishes, Amigo," said Alfredo.

"Adios, compadre," said Hermin.

Cameron the Otter –
Supermarket Employee

Supportive, Motivating, & Powerful

The next shoe he bumped into was Cameron the Otter.

"Are you all right?" Asked Cameron the Otter.

"I'm good, I'm just a little Thirsty," said Hermin.

Cameron said, "I'll give you a complimentary soft drink on the house."

Hermin said, "Thank you so much."

"My pleasure," said Cameron.

Hermin asked Cameron what his job was and, in three words, what best describes it.

Cameron said, "I'm a Supermarket Employee. I manage inventory and assist customers and staff. My three words are: Supportive, Motivating, and Powerful."

"Much thankful," said Hermin.

"Anytime," said Cameron.

Howie the Dolphin - Gardener

Favor, Diligence, & Speed

Now Hermin had enough Air for Two more encounters under water before his air tank runs out.

"Got to make it count," said Hermin.

Off he had swam into the ocean and was greeted by Howie the Dolphin.

"Hi, what's your name?" asked Howie the Dolphin.

"I'm Hermin the Ant," said Hermin.

"Pleased to meet you, Mate. I'm Howie the Dolphin. Nice to meet you too," said Hermin.

Hermin asked, "What is your job and, in three words, what best describes it?"

"I'm a Gardener. I upkeep the Gardens, Mate, cutting the hedges and grass. My three words are: Favor, Diligence, and Speed. Respect to you, mate," said Howie the Dolphin.

"Aye and you, mate," Said Hermin.

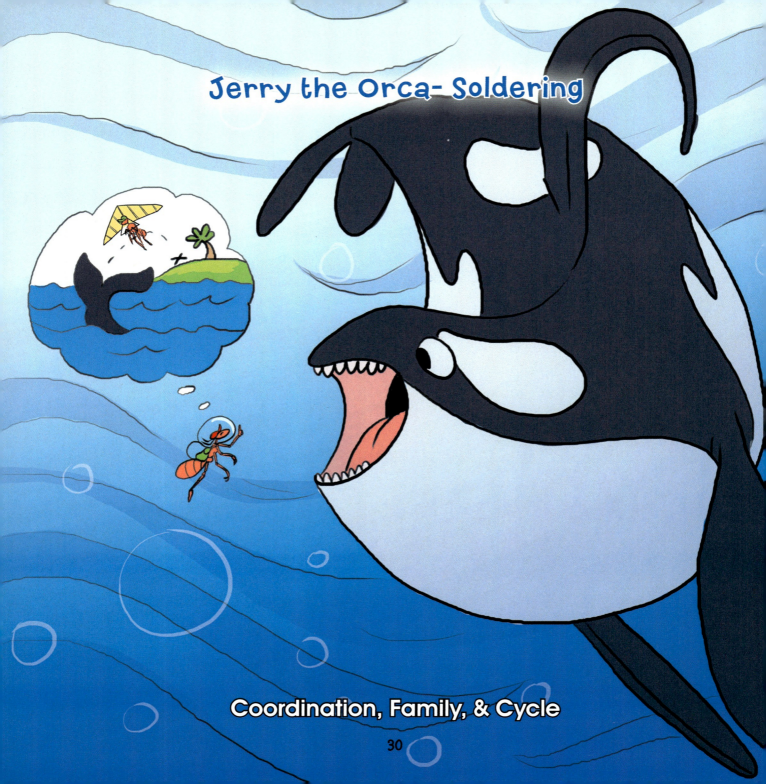

Now Hermin was almost out of air, and he was ways away from the coastline. That's when Hermin came up to Jerry the Orca.

"I'm Jerry the Orca."

"My name is Hermin, but I'm almost out of air."

"I'll Help you to the Surface," said Jerry the Orca.

Once Hermin got to the surface above Water, he took a deep breath of air in and said, "Thank you, Brother, you're a Lifesaver."

"That's what I'm here for," said Jerry the Orca.

Hermin asked, "What is your job and three words that best describe it?"

"I work in soldering, I solder computer chips onto motherboards. My three words are: Coordination, Family, and Cycle."

"Thank you, Jerry, for saving me," said Hermin.

"Anytime, Brother," said Jerry.

Hermin asked Jerry if he can launch him into the air toward the beach.

Jerry said, "It will be my pleasure."

So Hermin was tossed in the air then bicycle flipped by Jerry. As he was launched, he pulled out his little Hang glider and glided across the Ocean toward the Beach.

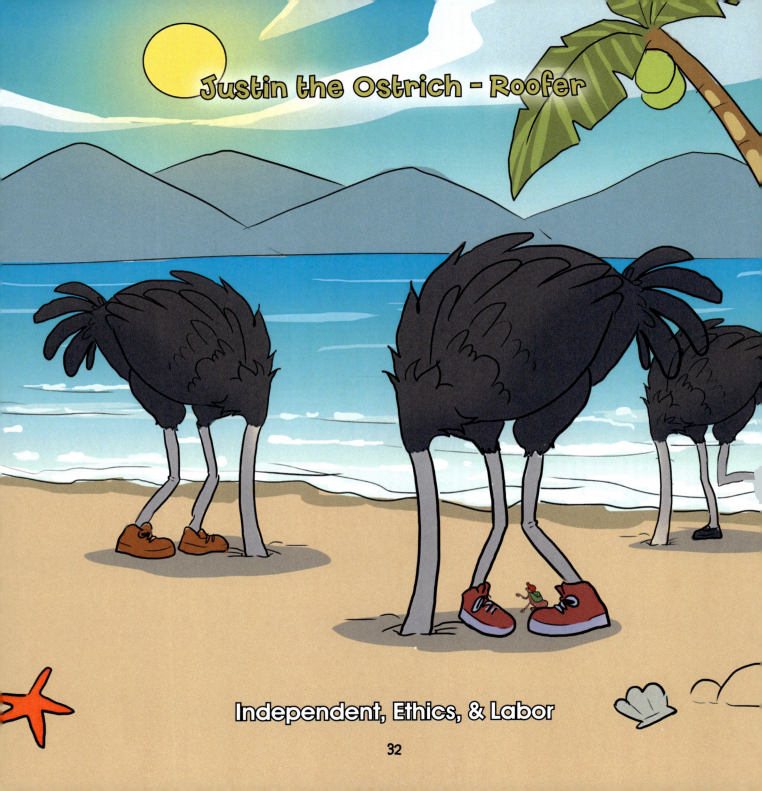

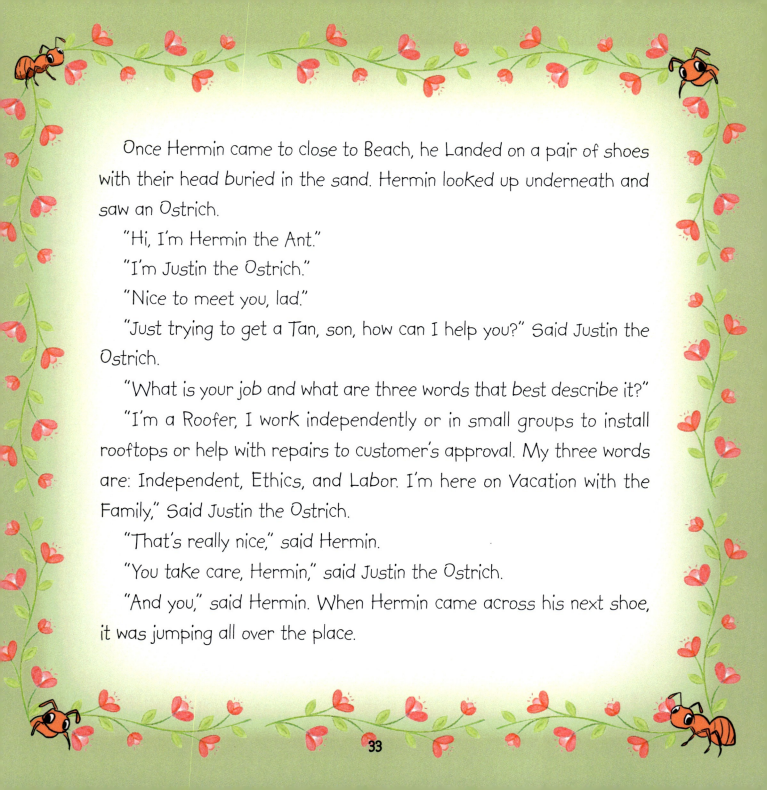

Once Hermin came to close to Beach, he Landed on a pair of shoes with their head buried in the sand. Hermin looked up underneath and saw an Ostrich.

"Hi, I'm Hermin the Ant."

"I'm Justin the Ostrich."

"Nice to meet you, lad."

"Just trying to get a Tan, son, how can I help you?" Said Justin the Ostrich.

"What is your job and what are three words that best describe it?"

"I'm a Roofer, I work independently or in small groups to install rooftops or help with repairs to customer's approval. My three words are: Independent, Ethics, and Labor. I'm here on Vacation with the Family," Said Justin the Ostrich.

"That's really nice," said Hermin.

"You take care, Hermin," said Justin the Ostrich.

"And you," said Hermin. When Hermin came across his next shoe, it was jumping all over the place.

Hermin had to time just right to land on this shoe. Hermin got onto the shoe and said, "Hi, how's it going? I'm Hermin the Ant, what's your name?"

"I'm Anthony the Monkey."

"Nice to meet you," said Hermin.

"It's my pleasure," said Anthony.

"What do you need, Hermin?" Said Anthony.

"Anthony, can you tell me your job and three words that *best* describe how you view your work?" said Hermin.

"I'm a Mental Health Care Worker, my three words are: Understanding, Knowledge, and Wisdom. By helping others in my field, I got to understand myself better," Said Anthony.

"That's very admirable and I appreciate you helping me," said Hermin.

"Your welcome," said Anthony. "Have a good day, Hermin."

"You as well, Anthony," said Hermin.

Kevin the Sloth- Bank Teller

Calm, Calculated, & Accurate

Hermin's next shoe was moving really slow.

"I'm Hermin the Ant, what's your name?"

"I'm Kevin the Sloth, pleasure meeting you, Hermin. How may I assist you?" said Kevin.

Hermin asked, "What is your job and what are three words that best describe it?"

"I'm a Bank Teller. I cash checks and handle money transactions. My three words are: Calm, Calculated, and Accurate. Thanks for checking on me," said Kevin the Sloth.

"It's all good," said Hermin. Now Hermin was starting to feel down because he felt like he wasn't getting were he wanted. Hermin wanted to find the meaning of John 3:16. He was using knowledge through his Dictionary to find the meanings of the words he encountered but felt like he was going in circles. "What to do?" said Hermin, then Hermin heard a calling saying, "Fear not little Flock." Hermin recognized that voice and immediately went and packed his bag and went straightforward to finish his Quest.

Now Hermin's next shoe was moving fast.

"Hello, what's your name?" asked Hermin.

"I'm Jessica the Squirrel. What's your name?" asked Jessica.

"I'm Hermin the Ant. Pleased to meet you, Jessica."

"Likewise," said Jessica.

"What is your job, Jessica? And what are three words that Best Describe it?"

"I work in IT and work in Customer Service for Management. My three words are: Positive, Organized, and Fruitful. I just finished work and off to Church for Christian Fellowship and Sunday Service. Would you like to come?" said Jessica. Hermin knew he was on the right path, once Jessica asked Him.

Hermin said, "I would Love to Go."

"Very Cool," said Jessica. So Jessica took Hermin to Sunday Service.

Now Hermin felt a positive inclination that came over him as soon as he entered the Church. Hermin Knew he was in the right place. Jessica went to go to the Front, and Hermin hopped on a shoe heading to the Altar. Hermin looked up and said, "Hi, I'm Hermin the Ant, what's your name?"

"I'm Pastor Raul the Rhino. Nice to meet you, Hermin."

"It's my pleasure," Said Hermin. "What is your Job and three words best describe it?"

"I'm Pastor of a Church and I preach the Gospel of Jesus Christ I hold Church Services every Wednesday and Sunday. My three words are: Love, Faith, and Truth."

Hermin Knew after hearing those specific words to ask the question about John 3:16.

Hermin asked, "Do you Know the meaning of John 3:16?"

"Yes," said Raul the Rhino, "it's found in the New Testament of the Holy Bible. John 3:16—'For God so Loved the world that He gave His only begotten Son, that whosoever believeth in Him should not perish but have Everlasting Life.'"

Hermin was deeply touched and asked, "Who is the Son?"

Raul said, "His name is Jesus Christ. Do you want to get to Know Him?"

Hermin said, "I would Love to."

Raul said, "Good, I will say a short Prayer with you before I give my Sunday Service today. It's about Jesus. Are you ready to accept him?" said Pastor Raul.

"Yes," Said Hermin.

Pastor Raul said, "Repeat after me: 'Lord Jesus, come into my heart, Forgive me of all my sins, show me love, guide me to your Light and righteousness, teach me all your ways through the Holy Spirit, fill me with purpose driven by you, Lord, so I can have eternal life and find Salvation through you. Lord Jesus, thank you for saving me. In Jesus's name, I Pray. Amen.'"

Raul the Rhino - Pastor of Church

Love, Faith, & Truth

Hermin felt inside and out the best he ever felt, and all the worrying and things that bothered Hermin were relieved and gone from him.

Pastor Raul said, "I'm very proud of you, Hermin, here's a Holy Bible to guide you through service. You won't need that Dictionary unless you're unfamiliar with a word. This Bible contains the Old Testament and New Testament. When we follow along about Jesus, we primarily look through the New Testament. I'm about to give service, Hermin Have a seat next to Jessica the Squirrel in the Front."

"I'd be delighted," said Hermin.

Now Pastor Raul went to the Altar and opened up his Bible and said, "Church, open your Bibles to John 8:12—'Then Jesus spoke unto them, saying, "I am the Light of the World: he that followeth me shall not walk in darkness, but shall have the Light of Life."' Next Turn to Matthew 5:16. Jesus said, 'Let your light so shine before men that they may see your good works, and Glorify your Father which is In Heaven.' Glad to have you following along. Now turn to John 6:35—'I am the Bread of Life. He that cometh to me shall never hunger, and he that believeth on me shall never thirst." Next turn to John 14:6. Jesus said, 'I am the way the truth and the life: no man cometh unto the Father, but by me.' Next Verse is Just above in John 14:1–3. Jesus said, 'Let not your heart be troubled. You believe in God, believe also in me. In my Father's house are many mansions: if it were not so I would have told you. I go to prepare a place for you. And if I go prepare a place for you I will come again, and receive you unto myself that where I am you may be also.'

"Glad you're all following along. Now turn your Bibles to Matthew 12:30. Jesus said, 'He that is not with me is against me, and he that is not with me scattereth abroad.' Next turn your Bibles to Luke 4:18-19. Jesus said, 'The spirit of the Lord is upon me, because he hath anointed me to preach the gospel to the poor. He hath sent to heal the broken hearted, to preach deliverance to the captives and recovering sight to the blind, to set at liberty them that are bruised, to preach the acceptable year of the Lord.' Next turn your Bibles to Mark 16:15-18, and Jesus said, 'Go ye into all the world, and preach the gospel to every creature. He that believeth and is Baptized shall be saved, but he that believeth not shall be damned. And these signs shall follow them that believe. In my name they shall cast out devils, they shall speak new tongues, they shall take up serpents, and if they drink any deadly thing, it shall not hurt them. They shall lay hands on the sick, and they shall recover.' Next turn to Luke 6:47-48. And Jesus said, 'Whosoever cometh to me and heareth my sayings, and doeth them, I will show you to whom he like: He is like a man which built a house and digged deep, and laid foundation on a rock: and when the floods arose, stream beat vehemently upon that house and could not shake it: for it was founded upon rock. But he that heareth and doeth not is like a man without foundation built his house upon the earth. Against which the stream did beat vehemently, and immediately it fell, and the ruin of that house was great.'

"Church, I would like to conclude the service. By telling you all that Jesus Loves you and wants you all to succeed and, most Importantly, in the end, be with Him in Heaven. This life is temporary but our eternal lives are forever. Jesus says in John 15:19, 'If ye were of the world the world would love its own: but because ye are not of the world, but I have chosen you out of the world, therefore the world hateth you.' Don't allow the world to get you down. Lastly I'd like to Close with John 16:33, and Jesus says, 'These things I have spoken unto you, that in me ye might have peace. In the world ye shall have tribulation: but be of good cheer; I have overcome the world.' God bless you all. Enjoy the rest of your day, Church," Pastor Raul said.

After the service, Pastor Raul said, "I can send you home by paper airplane?"

Hermin said, "That would be Great."

So Pastor Raul Constructed a paper airplane to send Hermin back home. When he finished, Hermin hopped onto the paper airplane and waved Goodbye to the Church and thanked Pastor Raul for witnessing to Him about Jesus Christ.

Pastor Raul said, "Share the Gospel of Jesus. It will do those you care about good."

"I will," said Hermin.

Pastor Raul said, "Count down 1, 2, 3, Take Off," and Pastor Raul Ran very fast with Hermin and threw the Paper Airplane. Hermin went deep in Air with the Paper Airplane. He was catching all the air currents keeping him afloat. Once Hermin got close, he popped a mini-flare to let his hive Know it's him. He jumped out of the plane and pulled his mini-parachute. As he hovered down, the other Ants looked up and said, "Hey. that's Hermin." "Hermin's back everyone," the other Ants shouted, a lot of them were excited to see Him.

As he landed, he was embraced by His Hive, and they wanted to know more about his Adventure; he shared with them about the Bible and what Jesus says in His words. As Hermin made his way to the Ant Queen Matlida, he was welcomed in the Royal Court.

Once inside, Hermin said, "Permission to speak your Highness?"

"Permission granted," said Ant Queen Matlida.

Hermin said, "Your Highness, I found the meaning of John 3:16 and also have the Bible to which it came from."

"Please read," said Queen Matlida.

"John 3:16—'For God so Loved the world, that He gave His only begotten Son, that whosoever believeth in Him should not perish, but have Everlasting Life.'"

Queen Matlida said, "Long ago, my Father shared this verse with me. It meant a lot to me then, it means a lot to me now."

Hermin asked, "Do you want to get to know Jesus Christ?"

"I would love to," said Queen Matlida.

"Repeat after me," said Hermin, "Lord Jesus, come into my heart, Forgive me of all my sins, guide me to your Light and righteousness, teach me all your ways through the Holy Spirit fill me with purpose driven by you, Lord, so I can have eternal life and find Salvation through you. Lord Jesus, thank you for saving me. In Jesus's name, I Pray. Amen." She felt uplifted and touched by saying the Prayer. The other Ants were also touched by the prayer and asked to receive Jesus, and sooner than later, the Ant Kingdom of Queen Matlida and her Ant people all turned their hearts to know Jesus Christ. In the End, Hermin witnessed all that was shared with Him and saved His Fellow People through the Blood, Love, and Testimony of Jesus Christ.

The End

"For God so Loved the world, that He gave His only begotten Son, that whosoever believeth in Him should not perish, but have Everlasting Life." John 3:16

Printed in the United States
by Baker & Taylor Publisher Services